the christmas tree story

Xulon Press
2301 Lucien Way #415
Maitland, FL 32751
407.339.4217
www.xulonpress.com

© 2021 by Danny Mishek

Illustrated by Megan Shumway

Paperback ISBN-13: 978-1-6628-2180-6
Hard Cover ISBN-13: 978-1-6628-2181-3
Ebook ISBN-13: 978-1-6628-2182-0

the christmas tree story

WRITTEN BY:

Danny Mishek

ILLUSTRATED BY:

Megan Shumway

MILL CITY PRESS

December arrives, social plans start to stir,
Knowing from past years it will be a blur.
Bringing excitement and great energy,
The start of the season begins with the tree.

With dinner parties, events, traditional obligations
Weekends and weeknights fill with celebrations.
Giving and sharing, spending more than one's worth
To celebrate blessings and a legendary birth.

IBER

THURSDAY	FRIDAY	SATURDAY
Shopping 2	Hang 3 X-mas Lights	Baking 4
8 Hockey!	Work 9 Party 6:00	Choir 10 Concert CUMC @7 ♪	Cookie 11 Exchange @11
14 Xmas Tea With Gus	Ship Gifts 15 To South Carolina	Pics 16 w/ Santa	Kid's 17 Pagent Rehersal	Wilson 18 X-mas Applewood 3:30
20 nding @ Oval	21 Secret Santa Exchange	Dog 22 Grooming ✂	Bell 23 Concert	Church 24 3:30 Mishek's 6:00	SANTA? ★ 25 Christmas! Johnson's @ 11

3

College kids wrap up finals and barter for rides
More laundry than clean clothes, luggage bursts on all sides.
Travel plans finalized—on the move or to host,
Budgets get stretched from coast to coast.

The tradition of the tree so different for each
The stories and memories have enchanted reach.
For some the journey is a drive out of the city
Visiting a farm where the trees are pretty.

Some support their local tree lots,
While others assemble their tree from a box.
There is no right and there is no wrong
This tree tradition is so very strong.

A local lot for us, Jolly Jack's was its name—
We ventured down each row, no tree was the same.
Claimed cut fresh each day, which I knew was a lie;
On the roof it got home with Jack's "2-mile-tie".

From Frasers to fakes and Balsams to firs—
It really comes down to what you prefer—
From short and stout to tall and skinny,
Filling the room or on a table as a mini.

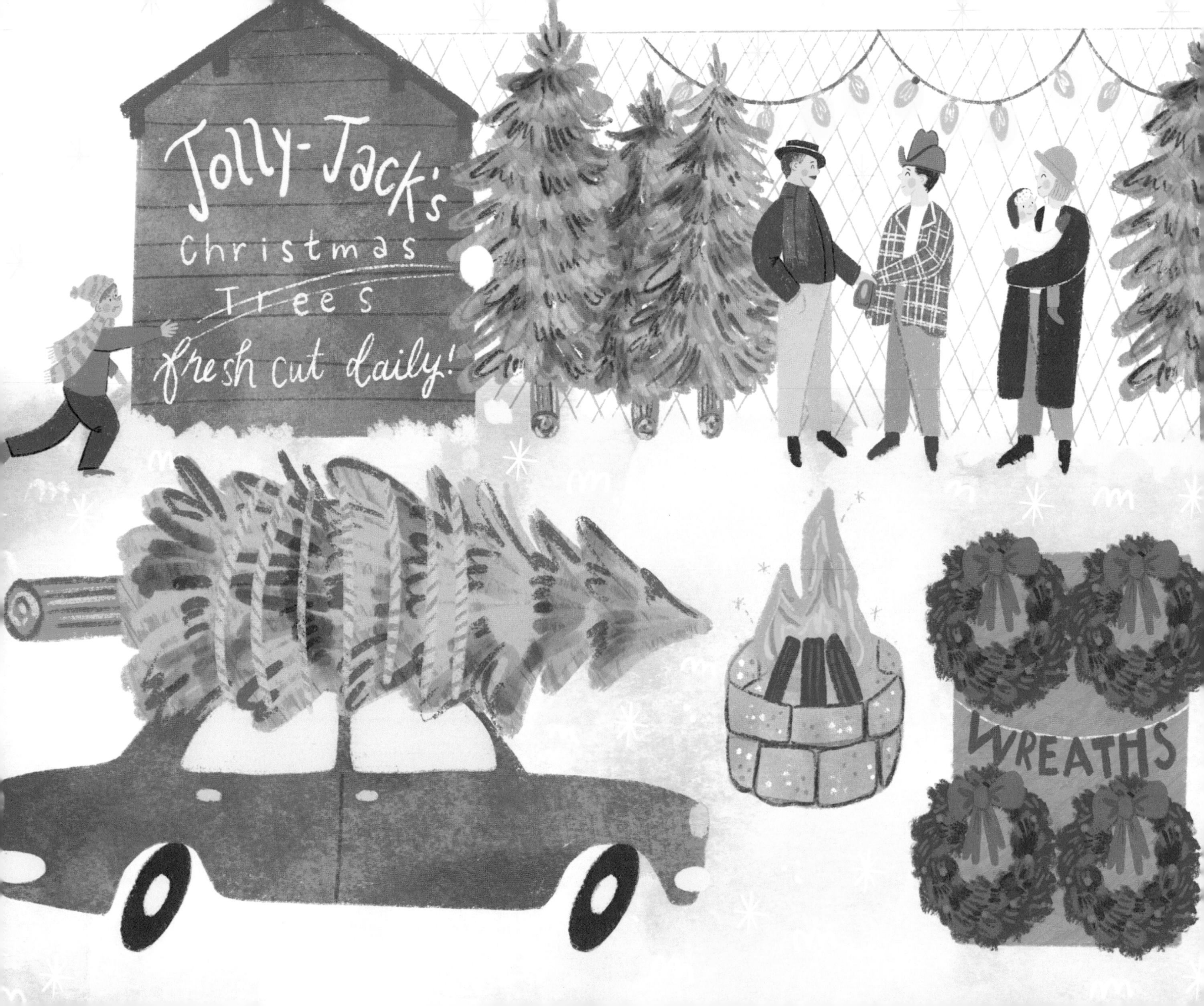
Jolly-Jack's
Christmas
Trees
fresh cut daily!
WREATHS

Once the tree is up and secured in its stand
Everyone gathers to hear the command.
Each tradition is unique like the falling snowflake
The celebration is yours, and what of it you make.

Before the tree is trimmed, the vision is clear:
It's a backdrop for pictures and wrapped Christmas cheer.
It will brighten the room and jumpstart the season,
Stemming talk of true meaning and the real reason.

As each tree stands tall anchored in place
It awaits its makeover, its fresh holiday face;
The firm lonely branches extend long and padded
Patiently waiting as the decorations get added.

The box of ornaments for all to see,
The first thought of many, "Is there room on the tree?"
From box to tree like paint to canvas
Each ornament gets hung as none can be missed.

Some knick-knacks are heavy, others are petite;
Some look so real, like candy to eat.
Hung with hooks or loops of string
Ready to be dangled like polished bling.

Tinsel and flocking with strands of lights,
Ornaments of the past hung with smiles of delight.
Memories from years past get put on display
As cookies and treats vanish from the tray.

A beverage is the classic start to trimming your tree;
A perfect time to share a cup of Christmas tea.
For others it's hot chocolate with marshmallows to add,
Maybe it's eggnog or a bourbon for dad.

The music selections are many and varied:
John Denver and the Muppets sing carols so merry.
Countless shared snacks, both salty and sweet
From cutouts and fudge to pepper-cured meats.

An orb of silver, a snowman with a hat,
A crocheted snowflake and a big fat cat,
A thimble, a bell and a yuletide log,
A first-grade picture, a skate and a bone for a dog.

The ornaments vary in shape and in color;
Received from friends, family and even little brother.
The memories of each trinket, a year or a trip,
A hobby, a pastime or a wine that you sipped.

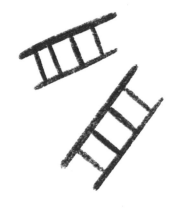

It's a lifetime collage that gets created each year,
Reminders of blessings and reasons to cheer.
Seeing the baubles displayed next to each other—
Alma Maters, sports teams and hand-me-downs from mother.

As the tree gladly accepts its sparkles and bulbs
Needles hit the floor as branches start to bulge.
Surrounded with raised arms and people tipped on their toes
The toy train gets set up and the engine horn blows.

Some ornaments are old and passed on for ages,
Others are new and at their launch stages.
Given with kindness from a student to a teacher,
A grandparent to a child or a choir member from a preacher.

Each decoration stands on its own—
Handmade, store bought, or custom glass blown.
Inscribed with landmarks or a trip at a glance,
From Savannah, Napa Valley or a church in France.

As memories are raised with a smile or a tear
Of fantastic travel or a lost loved one this year.
With the music and drinks starting to take hold
All are acting young again, no one feels old.

The tree in the window or corner of the room
Can fill the heart full, the entire body consumed.
Fancy or mismatched, whatever it may be
Or Grandma Elva's charming Charlie Brown tree.

As the box full of treasures approaches the end
One final task completes this holiday trend.
The tree topper of course, the icing on the cake,
The final step in the journey each tree must take.

Is it an angel, a cross or a bright shiny star?
Or newborn stocking caps that have made it thus far?
Once the tree is topped the people gather in bliss—
All are ready to welcome the joy of Christmas!

ACKNOWLEDGEMENTS

Special thanks to these people who have made Christmas so special for me. I am blessed to have these traditions. Mom and Dad, for every effort in celebrating a special birth while fitting five pounds of gifts, candy, and love into a three-pound Santa sack. I can still hear the bell ringing.

Grandma and Grandpa Mishek and Wilson, for making Christmas Eve (day and night) magical with family, food, billiards, music, gifts, and great energy. It was always the perfect way to set the stage for Christmas Day.

My in-laws, for accepting my brown dog and me in all of their family traditions. Receiving ornaments and decorating their tree has always been a memorable time for my family (Pickles and Ham).

Special thanks to these people that helped me get this story from my heart to paper.

Megan Shumway, for being an outstanding artist that captured every detail of my writing to make it relevant for all to enjoy. Megan's imagery moved me more than she will ever know.

Tess Ormseth, for giving me three draft edits that really made me realize I am a better talker than writer. I have a new and better appreciation for high school English teachers.

Todd Shern @ Rapit, for being the most helpful, resourceful, and compassionate person one could ever work with for printing and promotional needs.

My four children (Colten, Monterey, Arabella, and Kalifornia), for giving me spills, thrills, and chills at every life's turn. Even if I never sell a single copy, this book has been a success to me. It has allowed me to share the many blessings I have with you. You have all made Christmas special to me. May this endure for you and your families in the future.

To my lovely wife, Amelia, for being my tree-topper and my wine-sipper. For pushing me to be me and for never letting the sun set on our fun, passion, and love for life. You are the best "YES" I have ever received.

Snapshots
of
Inspiration

CPSIA information can be obtained
at www.ICGtesting.com
Printed in the USA
LVRC102353271021
701739LV00005B/49